W.H. Lord

A Sermon Preached on Occasion of the Fiftieth Anniversary of the Organization of the First Congregational Church in Montpellier, Vermont

SALZWASSER
VERLAG

W.H. Lord

A Sermon Preached on Occasion of the Fiftieth Anniversary of the Organization of the First Congregational Church in Montpellier, Vermont

Reprint of the original, first published in 1859.

1st Edition 2022 | ISBN: 978-3-37513-096-1

Verlag (Publisher): Salzwasser Verlag GmbH, Zeilweg 44, 60439 Frankfurt, Deutschland
Vertretungsberechtigt (Authorized to represent): E. Roepke, Zeilweg 44, 60439 Frankfurt, Deutschland
Druck (Print): Books on Demand GmbH, In de Tarpen 42, 22848 Norderstedt, Deutschland

A SERMON

ON OCCASION OF THE

FIFTIETH ANNIVERSARY

OF THE ORGANIZATION OF THE

FIRST CONGREGATIONAL CHURCH

IN MONTPELIER, VERMONT.

BY W. H. LORD, PASTOR.

A CITY WHICH HATH FOUNDATIONS.

A SERMON

PREACHED ON OCCASION OF THE

FIFTIETH ANNIVERSARY

OF THE ORGANIZATION

OF THE FIRST CONGREGATIONAL CHURCH

IN MONTPELIER, VERMONT,

JULY 25, 1858.

By W. H. LORD, PASTOR.

MONTPELIER:

E. P. WALTON, PRINTER.

1858.

SERMON.

Heb. xi., 10. A CITY WHICH HATH FOUNDATIONS.

In one of the noblest Psalms which the King of Israel struck from his inspired harp, there is a sublime apostrophe to the church at Jerusalem. In the opening strain he sings, *The Lord loveth the gates of Zion. His foundation is in the holy mountains. Glorious things are spoken of thee, O city of God.* And then he closes the hymn with a poetic declaration of the high honor which it brings to one to have been connected with its services, and to have been a resident of this glorious symbolic city. *The Lord shall count when he writeth up the people, that this and that man was born in her.*

The text I have selected is the apostle's expression of the same idea. It is descriptive of the earthly church. It is also prophetic of that immortal and equal society, the commonwealth of justified spirits, gathered by the Redeemer out of every kindred and nation. It is a type and symbol of that perfect state and city, ' whose citizenship is heavenly, whose charter is the infinite grace, whose title and right of freedom are faith in the Son of God;' whose eternal builder and protector, whose wall of fire and whose column of cloud, by day and by night, is the living God.

And while it is peculiarly true of the church in general; the church universal, visible and invisible, militant and triumphant; that it is a city which hath foundations, and to be a resident in it is the chief dignity and honor allotted to mortal man ; to share its promises and hopes and fortunes, his noblest blessedness : it may also be said of any particular church of Christ that it is a city which hath foundations, and so long as it rests upon its durable and strong *rock*, the gates of hell cannot prevail against it ; so long as it is built on Christ, and built up in him, there is no local church of the Redeemer of which glorious things shall not continue to be spoken.

We believe this church to be founded upon this eternal Rock. For a half-century it has proved the excellence and virtue of Him upon whom it has been built. It has witnessed days of rebuke and wandering and trial, but it has not left the corner stone. It has been assailed by foes within and without, but it is stronger to-day than ever. It has seen an end of theories and speculations and measures and institutions, and things that have aimed to supercede or weaken or destroy it. It has survived all antagonisms of men, all the oppositions of nature that have been brought to bear upon it, and still it stands to-day upon the same living foundation upon which it was built fifty years ago ; its numbers twenty-folded ; its reasons for confidence in Christ and God multiplied ; its faith and love as strong and clear as when they found their first organized expression.

A city which hath foundations—not commercial, not industrial, but moral, spiritual—that is the beautiful symbol of a christian church. And why may we not borrow the sublime imagery of the apostle, in which he paints the glory of the universal triumphant church, and use it to describe our own church, grown stronger, with the flight of years, and now numbering almost as many within the palace walls of heaven, as there are left on earth to fight the long, animating battle, for the same fadeless crown. The church lives, not more in its present, than in its absent and glorified members ; and while it enrolls on its catalogue the names of those who now stand before the sapphire-throne, as well as of those who are struggling onward and upward, we may well say that our foundation is in the holy mountains, or sing as did the Psalmist, of Jerusalem, *Glorious things are spoken of thee, O city of our God!*

A previous announcement of my subject makes no explanation or apology necessary for the direction which my discourse will take to-day. As you are well aware, the fiftieth anniversary of the organization of this church occurred on the 20th day of the present month. This is the first semi-centennial Sunday of its organized existence. It is well to take note of such cycles of time ; to compare our present and former condition ; to consult the record of providences and facts, to see how the hand of the Good Shepherd has led on his flock ; to learn what reasons we have for humility and what for praise ; what there is to dishearten and what to encourage, and to glean from the irrevocable Past, principles and motives to guide and cheer our hearts in the available Future. It was the usage of the Jewish church to keep every fiftieth year as a Jubilee, and hold high public festivities, and commence anew the whole course of social and religious life. Like the Olympiad of the Greeks and the Lustra of the Romans, the Jubilee of Israel was designed as a waymark in the history of the nation. On those semi-centennial periods, the people were wont to worship with peculiar and splendid services, and again reverting to the first principles of their social and religious organized life, to begin their work afresh with the results of past experience gathered up into lessons for future conduct and guidance. And I know of no reason why a christian church may not also have its recurring jubilees, and celebrate them, if not with equal magnificence, yet in a manner appropriate to the simple and divine beauty of its peculiar mission and services.

Of necessity my discourse will be desultory, pursuing rather a historical than a logical sequence, and running along with such statements of facts, and with such reflections, as are suggested in the history of the church. It will be like tracing a stream from its fountain head, along the course of its winding channel, now small and rapid, now over rocks, now through deep forests, now spreading itself out through rich and fertile meadows. There are two histories to any church—the external one of names, and events, and records, and statistics; and the internal one of thoughts, purposes, feelings, passions and principles. The one is found in books, and the other in minds and hearts and lives. The one is the dry channel, the bed of the stream, the geographical chart of its course; the other is the running water, with its murmuring music, or its swollen freshets, or its pouring torrent, coursing along banks set with beauty and foliage, and through a scenery glowing with light and variety. The external history is to be read, studied, compared, analyzed; the internal history is to be inferred and imagined. We would hardly care to read the former unless urged by some ulterior motive; but recently I heard a man say, that he would like to live over the latter. It would take him a day to read the one, it would take him fifty years to read the other. The first is a record of votes, of actions, of general results; the second is a long passage of toil, of fear, of hope, of faith, of love glowing, and love dimmed in the rage of controversy; of pains and afflictions, of body aches and heart aches; of temptations met, yielded to or overcome; of triumphs and songs of victory.

And it is to be regretted that even the records of this external history are not full; that they are always defective and unsatisfactory; not even perfect as a record of births, and deaths and baptisms. Still one cannot read them, imperfect as they are, without having the whole internal history of the church brought vividly to his mind. Even the list of deaths is eloquent, and opens a half-century of sorrows and trials; of parents mourning for children, and sons and daughters weeping over the ashes of fathers and mothers; and brothers and sisters, lifting their voices in a common grief. Nor is the catalogue of baptisms less touching and telling. In the old academy, in the old State House, in this church, on how many heads, now frosted with the snows of time, now sprinkled with the gray of autumn, have been poured the consecrating waters, with the uttered invocation " to Father, Son and Holy Ghost." With what pride and love, with what hope and prayers, have parental hearts been surcharged as they have, on the altar of this church, dedicated their children, and vowed them to Christ and his church,—and how now do they rejoice among the angels, at the fulfilled covenant, or wait and intercede for those who, twenty, forty, fifty years ago, they gave in faith, to the God of the Heavens and the earth.

Nor is the list of admissions in the church without a voice.—

> When God makes up his last account
> Of nations in his holy mount,
> It will be an honor to appear,
> As one new born and nourished there.

What spiritual experiences, what processes of conviction and sorrow, at the discovery of sin, have been gone through,—what doubts have been met and vanquished, what fears have been raised and quelled, what scruples and hesitations and distrusts, before even a single name of all that ample record has been entered upon the sacred roll. And how each name on that catalogue of many pages, speaks of the grace and goodness of God, through our Lord Jesus Christ, and testifies to the atoning life and death of the Son of the Highest,—and how they bring their separate and their united tributes unto the Savior of men, and join forever in a silent song of praise " *unto Him who hath loved us and washed us from our sins in his own blood.*' A noble company of near a thousand witnesses, stand upon that record, and they all bring their praise and thanksgiving up through the heart broken *miserere* of their penitence, to him that sitteth upon the Throne and to the Lamb. No matter what failures are there registered, the testimony of every person enrolled on the books of the church, is recorded for Christ, and it is the noblest association in which a man's name can be written; an association of intelligent, accountable and immortal beings, all recognizing their individual responsibilities to God; all avowing their supremest duty, their sublimest privilege—when they " avouch the great Jehovah, Father, Son and Holy Ghost, to be the object of their supreme love, and their everlasting obedience."

What worldly institution, founded upon mere temporal expediencies or ends, has such a retrospect, and such a future ? The walls and systems of all temporary policies, of all earthly organizations, shall fall down, not one stone left upon another, but here is a city that hath foundations. All true members in it are members of an eternal fellowship—citizens of a celestial state. They have written their names on the highest record, on which it is given man to write, and the ages of eternity will not efface the inscription. The tablet of the church is God's Book of Life.— The world may give us its associations and assume their superiority to the church, but the record of the latter outlasts the former, just as Eternity outlasts Time.

It would seem, then, that just in the proportion the church prospers among a people, and its moral and spiritual ideas are taught and received, does a State, or city, or town, become honored and great. It was the boast of the apostle Paul, when arrested at Jerusalem, and led off to prison by a rude soldiery, charged by false accusers, that he was not an Egyptian, the vile ringleader of a vile mob, but a veritable Hebrew of Tarsus, a city of Cilicia, " a citizen of no mean city," and, therefore, entitled to his freedom and to an audience of the people. The crowd respected his plea of defense, and standing on the castle steps he preached the sublime doctrine of his ministry. And yet this Cilician city was not so large as this. It stood upon the banks of a river no broader nor deeper than that which flows through our village. It was built almost in a day, and there was no material or commercial grandeur about it to command the homage of its apostolic Son, or to get for him the hearing and applause of the crowd. Whatever celebrity it had was derived from the superiority of its ideas, from the thoughts that had it for their birthplace, "from the religious culture of which it was the famed fountain head." It was its wisdom and its religion, that arrested the violence of the Jewish persecutor; encircled as with defensive armor, the dignity and freedom of the apostle, and raised it to the honor of being no mean city.

And so always the true foundations of a city, those which most resemble it to its heavenly pattern, are not its extent, its wealth, its luxury, its ambitious houses, its commerce and its sports; but they are the spirit and temper of the people, the ideas that form, direct and regulate, the reverence for religious things, the strict consecration of divine institutions and ordinances. They are in the thoroughness and discipline of education, in the abundance of charity, the purity of manners, the sincerity of social life, the moral and Christian virtues that grace womanhood and adorn manhood. It is not houses, and shops, and factories, and public buildings, that make a noble community—but plant your foundations deep and broad in the moral, in the religious natures of men; train and develop their rational and their immortal powers: and then shall you " be citizens of no mean city." It is men—women—with true ideas of God and Christ, and with profound reverence for divine institutions, and for all that elevates and blesses the minds, hearts and souls of a State, that are its genuine, deepest, best foundations.

This principle, so apparent in its statement, practically so little thought of, was recognized by the early settlers of this community. This village had been settled about ten years, and was already collecting a considerable population, when the principle began to act as a distinct motive, upon the minds of its residents. They came to the conclusion that the correctives of religious influence, and restraint, and ideas, were essential to elevate the character of the community. Acted upon by the motive of immediate utility, and also moved by those wants and necessities of the spiritual nature, which are always seeking satisfaction though often finding none, it was voted, January 16, 1800, at a legally warned meeting of the town, to choose a committee of three persons to employ a teacher of religion, to be compensated out of the town treasury. The idea of what were the true foundations of a civilized community then first found its expression in this place. In 1800, the town *voted* that religion was the essential thing to the welfare and prosperity of the place. Men must have the ideas and the principles of religious responsibility, of accountability to God, or there is no protection to the individual character, and no security to the public welfare. Divine ideas of duty, of privilege, of truth, of immortality, must be taught and held if we would fashion an earthly community according to our inbred and instinctive conception of what a community ought to be. A lively sense of religious responsibility must run into all our actions, whether personal or social. It is the obligation of citizenship to shape our actual society and its institutions, by the models of the Divine Word. That obligation was recognized in the vote to which I have alluded.

Before this time, as occasion had required, the inhabitants availed themselves of the services of the first minister in the town of Berlin. He preached at funerals, and in one instance on Sunday, in a house in the village. That minister, settled in the town of Berlin sixty years ago last January, a man of education, of sensibility and native power, still lives ; and but three weeks ago he spoke with a vigor not abated by three score years of service for his Master, in our vestry. And it was with a new interest that I looked upon his venerable form and features, when I remembered that his voice was the first that proclaimed Christ crucified in the houses of this village.

Upon the instruction of the town, the committee proceeded to employ a religious teacher. And after various unsuccessful attempts they engaged the Rev. CLARK BROWN for a year. This was before the organization of any society or church, and no records have been kept of his ministry. But from what can be gathered from the tradition of the elders, it would seem that Mr.

Brown was a preacher of considerable talent, but not of very sound religious views. He was inclined to the Unitarian theories, and however much interest there might have been in his ministrations at first, it soon subsided, and he was left to preach to very meagre and unsatisfactory audiences. And whatever might be the natural or the Christian patience of the man, it was so largely drawn upon as to be exhausted. In six months after he was employed, he took occasion on one Sunday to tell some very homely truths about the people. He charged upon them their faithlessness to religious duties, and painful disregard of public worship. He might have said some very earnest and severe things, and stirred up the people to a more just appreciation of their miserable sinfulness. At least the effect of the sermon was immediate and decided. After service, several of the leading and prominent citizens of the town assembled in a neighboring inn, and voted to pay Mr. Brown for the remaining six months of his engagement, and to release him from any further duties of the ministry in this place. A thing both well done and quickly done ; for a people often find it easier to pay arrearages and dismiss ministers, than to reform themselves or go regularly to church all day.

After this summary dismission of Mr. Brown, the town appears to have forgotten in fact, that religion was the only true foundation of its public security and its individual character. For eight years there was no regular religious worship. A writer in one of the periodicals of the day says of them, in a communication made in 1809 : "They were not disposed to encourage attention to religious concerns, and no religious order was observed in the place for a number of years. The inhabitants, as might be expected, became generally dissipated, and a deplorable state of morals was the result. The Sabbath was used only for purposes of amusement, convivial entertainments, trading and gambling." Of course that is always the result, and worse, too, than that, when men knock out the foundations of a Christian city, and think they can live without God. The same causes have produced similar effects a million of times. No city, no town, no community, no person, has any solid foundation of virtue or of security, that is not formed after the pattern of Christ, and built up in all the order of his Gospel.

But the germs of a better life, the elements of a purer society, though slumbering and overgrown, were not quite dead. Again in 1804, a number of inhabitants met, and resolved to take all reasonable measures to enforce the laws of the State, respecting the observance of the Sabbath, and to attend meetings every Sunday at the Academy, and when destitute of preaching, to sing and read sermons. Twenty-nine persons signed that resolution.—The germ was trying to break through its hard shell. The meetings were held, but even then for nearly three years more, prayer was not heard in any family in the village, and very rarely in their assemblies on the Sabbath. In 1807, a preacher was employed who left the same year.

But such a state of things could not continue in a place that was soon to become the political centre of the State. As yet, men had been trying to build a superstructure without paying any attention to the foundations. They were laying the sills and beams of the house on the sand, and while they were practically finding out the insecurity of that method, they had not yet got the full idea of the essential thing. There remained for the Providence which had great designs for the place, to teach its inhabitants that except the Lord build the house, they labor in vain that build it ; except the Lord keep the city, the watchman waketh in vain. The necessity of the community became stark, staring want. It could not be hid from the eyes of any one.—The Gospel must come in to establish order, to moderate and check passion and vice. The Sunday must be transformed from a holiday to a holy day, and the people must think of eternal things, if they would have any system, and harmony, and healthful growth in temporal things. The prayerless meeting ; the occcasional religious instruction, were insufficient. The few good men and women who knew the difficulty and its remedy, were powerless, and must wait until the people in general had learned wisdom from adversity, from the very reaction of an irreligious disorder. The time was at hand for a decided change for the better, or ,for determining the course of this place to be downward and destructive. On the 12th day of April, 1808, the action was taken, which, under God, turned the course of events, and gave an upward movement to the society. Eighty-three men, all the leading and best men of the village, met and organized themselves into a religious society by the name of the " *First Congregational Society in Montpelier.*" As they say in their recorded declaration, "Impressed with the importance of religious institutions to society in general, and to ourselves as men—and taking into consideration the unsettled state of such institutions in this part of the country, and the necessity of uniting in religious opinions and harmony, we do hereby agree to form ourselves into a religious society, under the following regulations."

That was a noble declaration, made under a dire necessity. It has been kept to this day. It is the organization under which we now act. * The first regulation under it, was also a noble pledge. " 1. We pledge ourselves to each other, (say these eight-three men,) that we will (laying aside trifling differences,) according to our abilities, maintain regular meetings in our society and contribute to the support of preaching and to maintaining a regular clergyman in this society." Of that number, nearly all are passed from earth. Five only remain with us. You may be curious to know their names. I shall not hesitate to gratify the sentiment. First on the list, and first in order, is the name of GEO. WORTHINGTON; next in order, NATHAN JEWETT; next, JOSEPH HOWES; next, JONATHAN SHEPHERD; and last, SAMUEL GOSS. These tarry with us yet, and may they all

* See Appendix.

return late into heaven ; when called from earth, may they all enter the city of eternal foundations, " whose builder and maker is God."

April 27 ; this society held its first meeting under its organtion and choose SAM'L GOSS a committee for the purpose of contracting with a clergyman. May 27, a meeting was warned to see if they would employ the Rev. CHESTER WRIGHT through the ensuing year. June 4, voted to employ Mr. WRIGHT for six months. At the end of the year, June 24, 1809, the society voted to unite with the church in calling Mr. WRIGHT to settle in the gospel ministry in this place, and to give him $350 for the first year, $375 for the second, $400 together with the use of a convenient parsonage, annually, after the second year, so long as he shall continue to be their minister.

This is the first indication on the society's books of a church. And now we go back a little to the time of its organization.

The organization of the society was the first step toward building this community on a true and lasting basis. And still, it is apparent to every reflecting mind, that however many worthy and benevolent objects a society may accomplish, it is rather an external institution than an internal. It is an association of persons who are externally working to introduce and sustain right ideas and principles, rather than a company who recognize their obligations to God and Christ, and are trusting in the merits of Christ's death, and in the power of His word and spirit to be and to live better, holier, purer. It is a moral rather than a spiritual institution ; and while not doing away with the necessity for a church, makes that necessity more evident and imperative. It was found to be so in the case of this society. The church was its first practical result. The human institution was necessary as a precursor of the divine—a John the Baptist, heralding the personal Christ.

If religious institutions are important to society, and to us individually, as men, it was natural and necessary, too, for the preservation of the society, that a church should spring out of it, composed of those who would pledge themselves not simply to sustain preaching and the ministry of the divine word, but would pledge themselves also, to live according to that word, and to carry out its sacred and life-giving precepts in their daily practice. It was the legitimate process of an honest, sincere thinking mind, when convinced of the necessity of supporting religion, to go straight on to the personal avowal and duties of the gospel. The society said it is necessary to public security to sustain the doctrines of the New Testament. And what more natural thing than that consistent members of it, looking beyond any immediate public utility, should each say, It is equally necessary for me to adopt its principles as my principles, its God as my God, and its revealed redeemer as my Saviour. What more natural than that out of a body of near a hundred men, who witness to the general utility and necessity of religious institutions, some should be found who would wish to go further and declare their own personal allegiance to heaven, and bind themselves to duties and services that christianity prescribes, and aim to give a practical manifestation of their own confidence in those spiritual principles whose general promulgation is so vital to the community. Hence there arose some who said among themselves, if this gospel of Christ is so essential to be preached and supported, it is equally essential to be loved, received, obeyed. Its doctrines are not simply good for preaching. They are vital to a right living. They are the foundations of the city. They must be the foundations of our souls.

And thus thinking, and moved by the heavenly impulse, they gathered themselves together and were formed into another society,—a *society* relying upon the divine aid and spirit; confessing and adoring the divine Redeemer, and aiming to carry out into daily life the vital doctrines and rules of Christ, and to discharge responsibilities and obligations they had theoretically recognized as essential. They aimed to restore religion to its throne in their hearts, and planted a church for its nurture, against which the gates of hell shall not prevail. They deemed that Christ was as necessary to the individual as to society, and that He should be admitted into their hearts and lives as a welcome guest, as a life-giving Saviour, as a Supreme Ruler, and that His church was the great helper and bond of their spiritual obligations, and had clear claims upon their personal membership and service: that His church is the only organization for giving practical effect and triumphant power to the deepest truths of God's word; and, therefore, urged by a conviction of duty and by the best motives of the divine spirit and word, they asked of the neighboring churches and ministers, to embody and organize them into a church of Christ. Accordingly, on the 20th July, 1808, three months after the institution of the society, seventeen persons,—eight men, nine women,—were organized into a church of Christ.* Three of that number are still living and are present in this house to-day, and one of them was the first clerk of the new church. At the first communion thereafter, twelve more persons were admitted to the church by profession, and but one of that number is now living.

The worship of the church was in the old Academy, and was conducted by Mr. WRIGHT. On the fifth day of May, 1809, the youthful church received a letter from the church in Falmouth, Mass., expressing their congratulations, and in token of their love and fellowship, presenting a " set of vessels for the Holy Communion." At the same meeting the church voted to give a call to Mr. WRIGHT. Before the ordination of Mr. WRIGHT, which occurred on the 16th day of August, 1809, and on the day of his ordination, there were baptized fifteen children. Some of those children are before me. Some of them are in the heavens.

The effects of the steps already taken in respects to the religious interests of the village, were decided and permanent. It was soon demonstrated how much more effective and useful is a

* See Appendix.

complete ecclesiastical organization, than any random individual or social activity. The little church, with its newly elected pastor, its regular services, and its scriptural ordinances, its doctrine, fellowship, breaking of bread and prayers, became a *power* in this community. There was a life in it, not fitful nor spasmodic, but constant and divine, stedfast and earnest. There was one thing strongly in favor of the beneficial action of the church. The people had received but little religious instruction ; they were free from those inveterate sectarian prejudices and opinions, which always spring up in the pathway of ignorant or bigoted or denominational preachers. The preamble to their society rules, shows how completely they were inclined to merge all trifling differences, and come to worship together under one ministry. They were harmonious in their general religious views. They had had a specimen of the preaching of an errorist, and were satisfied with it. There was no hungering nor thirsting after fanciful doctrines, and sparkling religious theories. They needed some firm, consistent, elevating, divine system and truth, to stem the destructive tides, that were sweeping out their security, their morality and their respectability, and they wanted just what they needed. Their wishes run paralell with their necessities. They needed foundations for a christian city, and they had learned that all other foundations are vanity and vexation, and they now were prepared generally to receive and build upon the chief corner stone—the *Rock* of Divine Truth.

The first pastor of the church says of the state of religion at the time of the organization of the church and subsequently, "The public examination of the candidates for church membership, together with the solemn transaction of professing faith in the several articles of the religion of Christ, and entering into covenant with God and with each other, appeared to affect the minds of numbers, and several were soon after hopefully brought to embrace the Gospel. Here and there a solitary individual was powerfully wrought upon, and brought to the knowl-

.edge and love of Jesus, and the church received additions at almost every communion till the time of my ordination.'' Several were converted in the ensuing autumn, and united with the church some time in the winter. In the following spring, just as the face of nature was being renewed, and the earth was bursting with the germs of flowers and fruit, and putting on her queenly robes, and preparing her annual tribute of praise to the Lord and Giver of her life,—the divine seed, which had been sown in the moral soil, began to germinate and reveal the power of that divine life which quickened and vivified it. On Sunday, the 27th of May, 1810, the assembly was larger than ever before known on a like occasion, and remarkably attentive. The evening conference beheld the unusual sight of a thronged and crowded auditory. After the usual service of remarks, prayer and singing, a young man rose and wished to address the assembly. His emotions choked his utterance, and when at length he found voice to speak, he informed them that he had given up his opposition to the truth, and had yielded to the divine influence that drew him to the Savior. He confessed and mourned his sin. · He was followed by a friend, who expressed himself in a similar manner. The effect of their appearance was wonderful. It struck the magnetic cord of religious sensibility till it vibrated, so that while tears flowed from every heart, yet joy sparkled in the brimming eyes of the friends of Zion, and their souls seemed to triumph in the faith of the divine blessing. Monday was still as the Sabbath. On Tuesday evening, at the church conference, eight or nine young men avowed themselves for Christ. The progress of the work was rapid, but without disorder or any wild excitement. The interest continued till September, when it gradually subsided, with some intervals of transient reawakening and some new instances of conversion. It was confined almost wholly to the village, consisting at that time of only sixty families, and the church was increased in the first two years of its existence to the number of seventy. Very many of those who but

a little while before had united themselves to the society and
signed that remarkable statement, declaring that the Gospel was
essential to them as a community and as men, were led to yield
their personal homage to the Redeemer, and in His church to try
to apply the general doctrines they professed. The whole choir,
then led by a venerable member of our present audience, all became members of the church, and it might have been said of the
church then, as David sung of the ancient Zion, *As well the
singers as the players on instruments shall be there.*

In two short years, the testimony is universal, a great change
passed over the society. The city which hath foundations, whose
builder and maker is God, was beginning to rear its walls, and
palaces, and temples, and to be inhabited with a divine glory.—
In family after family, the worship of the true Jehovah was estab-
lished, and morning and evening sacrifice was regularly offered
in the name of Jesus. Men of unbelieving and sceptical sentiments became impressed and sobered. Young men of dissipated
habits became industrious and devout. The streets no longer
echoed with ribaldry and profaneness ; social life and intercourse
were greatly refined and improved. Generous charity, compre-
hensive courtesy, true hospitality, gave a freshness, an amen-
ity, a mutual interest and affection, a pure flavor and relish to social exchanges and recreations never known before, and it seemed
as if the placid and beneficent spirit of christianity had descend-
ed to hover over and to dwell in a place once so troubled and
distracted.

The influence of this interest still continued, or rather, and it
seems the more proper and the more in harmony with the laws of
the spiritual kingdom of Christ to say, the principles upon which
the church was built, the principles of religion, which found
expression in the organization of the society, attended and
blessed by the Divine spirit, kept on working and producing their
genuine and legitimate results. I love to think of those principles, still operating, and acting with more or less urgency on the

minds of the people, as they awake to their consideration and as
the church is faithful and earnest in their inculcation. The
faithful ministrations of the pastor, and the prayers of the church,
kept alive in the minds of men the lessons of divine truth. In
the three years subsequent to 1812, over thirty persons united
with the church; and then again, from 1816 to 1820, the records
would indicate a general seriousness and an honest consideration
of religious duties. In that circle of four years, 142 persons were
admitted to the fellowship of the church. At no time in the history of Mr. WRIGHT's ministry, was there any remarkable moral
sterility. The influences of divine grace and truth were steady
and effective. The special times of religious interest were not
followed by drought and reaction. There were changes of tides,
periods of its flood and years of its ebb; but the history of the
church was strictly in accordance with the ordinary course of
spiritual laws. In 1826, Nov. 27, the Sunday School was estab-
lished by vote of the church. In 1827 there was another spring
tide of divine influence and religious zeal and love, and more than
seventy were led to the acknowledgement of their duties and relations to God. And again in 1830, there was a general religious interest. The church was almost daily enlarging, and from
a little band had come to be a great assembly of the professed dis-
ciples of Christ. In December, 1831, occurred the dismission of
Mr. WRIGHT, after a laborious and successful ministry of twenty-
one years, in which the church had grown from absolutely the
least of all seeds, from almost or quite nothing, *to be*, and then to
become a great tree, of wide-spreading branches, filled with fruit-
age and blossoms, the fresh opening bud of religious experience,
the full-blown flower of christian hope, and the strong, hardy,
ripe, mellow fruit of a matured christian character and life. During the ministry of Mr. WRIGHT, 428 persons were admitted to
the church, an average of more than twenty per year, and of
more than three at each communion. But the fruits of his
ministry are not to be estimated by numbers, but only by the

moral measurements of eternity. Whatever controversies might have disturbed his peace or troubled the closing days of his ministry among his people, yet never a tongue, in all the numberless allusions that I have heard made to him, has spoken aught but in respect of his character and admiration of his ministry. Even those who questioned the wisdom of his course, have never impugned the sincerity or the purity of his motives and his life. If the zeal of the Lord's house had eaten him up; if he regarded the honor and peculiar sacredness of the Christian covenant and professsion, with a careful and ever watchful jealousy; if the church was to him dearer than the apple of his eye; if he felt that no earthly institution or order should usurp in men's thoughts or affections the place that was due only and altogether to the glorious city of his God; if he believed that she furnished an arena wide enough for the exercise of all human gifts and powers, and if he oppugned with warmth and ardor principles and systems, that he feared were subtracting from the crown of his master some of its lustre, and from the diadem of the church some of its prerogatives and titles, he certainly stands unimpeached before the tribunal of Heaven. It was the excellence, the purity, the power, the permanence of no trifling, or inferior, or unworthy object for which he was solicitous, and we wonder not that he who preferred Jerusalem above his chief joy, he whose tongue would have forgotten its gifts, and whose hand would have lost its cunning, rather than the least injury or defacement should come to the loved object of his prayers and his toils, should view with painful jealousy, and attack with a natural and generous impetuosity, the apprehended evil.

Mr. WRIGHT was a warm-hearted, true-hearted man: frank and fearless, sincere and honest, transparent as the air, liberal and generous to a fault. As a preacher, he was surpassed by none in the State. As a pastor, it would be impossible to overstate his worth and excellence. To relieve necessity, to comfort sorrow, to assuage grief, to lift burdens from mens' shoulders and carry them himself, was his delight. His benevolence and charity were singularly strong and massive virtues. He loved men with a warm, unselfish love. He loved to whisper words of Christ into the ears of the dying, and his noiseless footfall oft brought a living and abundant sympathy into the chambers of the sick and afflicted. No duties of his ministry were too lowly for his performance ; no sacrifices and self-denials too great to be made for the good of others. With all his zeal, he was a man of judgment. His counsel and advice were sought and esteemed. He was strict in doctrine, kind and decided in discipline, watchful and prayerful. Even to this day, the living power of his ministry is seen and felt in all this community, and his memory is kept in the hearts of many, fresh and sacred—fragrant and perfumed with the savor of a deep, deathless devotion to the cause of his Master. The church, nay, the village of Montpelier, is indebted to him, under God, for many of those principles and sentiments, and generous, hospitable, social traits, and kind brotherly feelings, which have distinguished its society. Underneath all the frivolities and conventionalities of her modern life, there is a strong, blessed undercurrent of human sympathies, and effective feelings of social interest and life, which have their source in the influence of his ministry. His record of labor and love, of care and solicitude, of charity and devotion, of sympathetic ministration, and faithful, earnest instruction, is above. But to-day we would not forget to speak of him who for nearly half the history of this church was its chosen pastor, whose heart was wrapped up in its welfare, and who now looks down from the glorified assembly of heaven, to share in our joys at the further triumph of those holy principles to which he consecrated his life, and whose ineffaceble virtue was attested in his ministry, and is proved in the sacred services of this occasion.

In the course of the ministry of Mr. WRIGHT, two events occurred, materially affecting the interests and prosperity of the church, that should be mentioned in passing. The society had

been without any place of worship of its own until this edifice
was built. It had occupied the Academy as a place of worship
until 1810, and after that held its assemblies in the old State
House, until 1820. Its present house of worship was completed
during that year, and has been occupied ever since, with several
revisions and changes, for the public service of the church.—
And by a singular Providence, the State, to which the society was
indebted for a place of worship for ten years of its early history,
is now dependent upon the society for its house of General Assembly. From the beginning, there seems to have been a practical, external union between the State and this church, and a mutual dependence and interchange of hospitalities. The second
event was the formation of the Methodist church in this village.
By a wise construction of human nature, and a kind arrangement
of Providence, it is impossible that all men should see, and feel,
and think alike, in regard to external forms and organizations
and policies. Agreeing in the essentials of religion, it is a necessity of nature that they should differ in non-essentials. The
forest must have its various trees, whose diversified figures and
size and color and foliage and fruit and flowering make up the
singular beauty and glory of natural scenery. So the church
must have its differences of worship and forms, a divine unity in
connexion with an endless variety. Thus it addresses men of all
castes and of every degree of culture and position. For the general interests of religion, and for the particular advantage and
prosperity of this church, nothing could have been more favora-
ble than the organization of the church of another denomination
in this village. The whole field had become too large to be
reached by one class of laborers. It needed, then, that others,
differing from us only in name and methods, should enter into it,
to speak to a mass of hearers that we could not reach, and to
subserve the cause of Christ in quarters that were beyond our influence. Whatever small and contemptible jealousies might at
times spring up in the operation of the different churches, would

necessarily all disappear under the reflection of an intelligent judgment. The churches of various denominations can work together, for the same ends, with less of rivalry than those of the same denomination, and it is a far happier thing for the interests of religion that the one universal church has its distinct and various branches and forms of discipline, than if it was given over to the inaction, to the dead level, or to the terrible bigotry and despotism of a dull and dreary uniformity.

After an interval of nine months, the church was supplied with another pastor. Mr. HOPKINS occupied the pulpit but three years and a half, when his resignation was rendered advisable by the state of his health. Near the close of his ministry, a new Congregational church was formed by members of this church, dismissed with reference to that object. In the course of his labors here, forty-eight persons were received into the church. It has been stated that his dismission from the society was caused in part by his apprehension of the effect of the new measure movement, to which at that time the church seemed disposed to commit itself. Be that as it may, I find from the records that immediately upon his leaving, the Rev. Mr. BURCHARD, a noted revivalist, was invited to hold one of his protracted meetings in this church. For more than forty days he labored in this village, and doubtless with many good results. Still it is apparent that the good was accomplished only at a tremendous cost. The regular services of the church, and the regular duties and labors of life, were broken up, and in some cases dispensed with altogether. Business was in a great degree suspended. The wildest excitement and extravagance took the place of sobriety of deportment and calm, intelligent reflection and action. Mens' minds and hearts were stimulated with unhealthful motives, were urged to avowals they were not prepared to make; and religion, a quiet, beautiful spirit of faith and love, and of faith working by love, was transmuted into the passion of an hour or the spasm of a day. Unintentionally, the holiest things were travestied—false ideas of conversion, as if it were some mystical, magical change, and of a religious life, as if it were a momentary fever, or the sudden thrill of sensibility, were inculcated. The mystery of divine influence and operation was parodied. The doors of the church were swung wide open, and while the fever was on, in the space of a short month and a half, more than a hundred and twenty-five professed their faith in Christ. It is such scenes, my brethren, in which men attempt to do the work of God, that are most fatal to the virtue, and faith, and the activity of the church. And had it not been for the strong undercurrent of religious principle, flowing down from the fountain head of the church, and identified with its history and its former ministry, such a passionate excitement, such a galvanized, spasmodic action, must have proved fearfully injurious, if not destructive. But a city which had foundations, however shaken it might be by such a moral earthquake, was not doomed to be destroyed. It had recuperative power, and when the flaming words, the spiritual stimulants, the external passion, ceased to be felt, the church gathered itself from its reaction of excitement, took home the lessons of an instructive experience, and set itself to the work of discipline and correction.

Of course after the departure of such an exciting preacher, the church would find it difficult to settle down to the regular ministrations of the divine word, or to find a pastor who would unite their suffrages. For a year thereafter, the society was afflicted with seventeen candidates, a number sufficient to have furnished a half dozen superior ministers. At length a call was given to Mr. B. W. SMITH, and accepted. He labored to the general satisfaction, but under very great disadvantages from ill health, for four years, when he resigned his pastorate. During his ministry eighty-two persons were admitted to the church.

In a few months after his dismission, Mr. GRIDLEY was installed as pastor, and continued in that responsible relation five years. The admissions to the church while he was here were forty-six.

The only event during his ministry of peculiar importance was the dismissal of several of the members of the church to the Protestant Episcopal Church, including one who was for a long time a faithful and efficient co-laborer with us, a superintendent of the Sunday School, and the not infrequent lay reader of sermons to this congregation ; a gentleman of education and piety, who became the first rector of that church in this village. It is not inappropriate to say that while we greet the success and prosperity of that society, and rejoice in its present healthful activity and enlargement, and recognize it, in its method and ways, as an efficient agent of Christ's Kingdom, we yet take peculiar satisfaction and pleasure in the remembrance that many of the principles and persons, which have given to it such animation and efficiency, were begotten and nurtured under the shadow of these walls. And it is almost with a maternal sentiment that we contemplate its origin, while with fraternal salutation we bid it to-day God speed in the work in which we are united, of raising this whole community to the level of the Gospel, to the principles of Christ, to the Kingdom of the blessed Redeemer. Diverse in form, the churches of this place are now constituted so as to address all shades of natural taste, and being one in spirit and in object, may yet tenfold their numbers and influence and become permanent radiating centres of living light, far and wide. It is their own fault if any mutual jealousy fetters their limbs and prevents the occupancy of their sufficient and wonderful heritage. The field is white to the harvest, and the Lord of the harvest bids us all work for a common and sacred end.

I have already, on a former occasion, adverted to the records of my own ministry among you; yet still, the occasion would seem to require some notice of its events. I came here in a time of division and controversy. With the dreams of youth and inexperience, I entered upon the hard toil of the ministry, in a disunited church, divided not in principle, not in vital sentiment, but in local policy and about persons. The records of the church

from that day to this are not mere statistics and notes and cata-
logues to me, but a life, a labor, a struggle, full of fears and ap-
prehensions, and encouragements, and joys, and hopes. On these
things one might naturally be garrulous ; but I forbear entirely.
1 will only say that God has blessed an unworthy and feeble ministry, and thank Him for the vast mercies that have followed the
course of our relationship. The short period of eleven years has
been filled with changes. I preach in the same house, but not to
the same audience that listened to my first sermon. Eighty re-
movals and sixty-three deaths in the society ; seventy dismissions
from the church and forty-three deaths in it—making a total of
two hundred and fifty changes since I began my work with you,—
have changed this church and society one-half. But yet while
we are daily losing, we are also daily gaining. There have been
one hundred and sixty-six admissions to the church—making a
net gain of fifty-six, and a considerable increase in the society.
There have been eighty baptisms. The church is now in an efficient state of organized action—its moral sentiments healthful,
its spirit of consecration and devotion revived. God has caused
His face to shine upon us and blessed us, and there is no reason
why the principles announced at the birth of the society and incorporated into its vital religious action, should not more thor-
oughly leaven and pervade the whole community. We have now,
in the religious interest which pervades the church, a specimen of
the divine power she should have and exert the whole time. We
work, and pray and wait, for larger accessions to the true church
and fold of the Redeemer—for those who were long ago baptized
at its altars—for those who for scores of years, through fair
weather and foul, have stuck by the society, and ever put their
shoulders to the wheel, never forgetful of the great principles of
the Gospel, but as yet not submitting to its personal claims.—
This church can now give her invitations with more earnestness
and force than ever before. She has a history of fifty years.—
She has tested the virtue of her everlasting foundations. She

has a roll of 924 members, of whom 364 are to-day in her earthly communion, and nearly 300 gone home to that happy harbor of God's saints,

> " Whose gardens and whose goodly walks
> " Continually are green."

And when we urge upon men the practical avowal of those principles they so cheerfully acknowledge and heartily sustain, our entreaty is enforced by a great cloud of witnesses; by the voices of the living and the dead; by the united voice of a large and illustrious throng of near a thousand members. We ask them to enter and become residents of a city which hath foundations, proved to be solid and safe by the experience of the best and wisest, by the facts of Providence, by the passage of generations, by the testimony of history, events, persons. We stand upon high ground, upon the rock of immutable truth, upon the foundation of imperishable principle, upon a platform on which have been planted the feet of myriads of the saintliest men, upon the deep convictions of human want and instinctive aspiration; and while we point to the records of the past, as evidence of the power and necessity of religion, we point you to the future as the alone scene of its joys and victories. If the church in the future be only faithful to its own history and its own principles, it shall yet give practical efficiency and triumphant success to the sacred lessons of Divine Truth. It shall be an organization that shall teach to coming generations, that the life is more than meat; that the soul is too precious to be bartered for the world. It should set wide open to all true penitents and seekers after life and immortality, the gates of that city whose foundations are builded and made by God. It shall be the means for unfolding and nourishing our capacities for morality and piety. It shall be the nursery of all goodness, the school of the purest graces, the temple for prayer and praise, the holy mountain of which glorious things will be spoken.

The time has come and now is, when this community perceive that we are just as distinctly required to recognize, love and obey and worship God, as to supply our physical necessities, as to improve our minds or cherish our social relations. This fundamental principle was incorporated into the very constitution of this society, when it declared in its organic article, that religion was essential to public interests and to individual men. The time is coming, we already forsee and greet its approaching dawn, when Christ's church, which is the great school and aid of our spiritual obligations, will have its claims on the personal respect and membership admitted by each one of you; when in a community like ours, receiving the dowry and heritage of christian principles and ideas, from the experience of the past, and from the teachings of the gospel and the Holy Spirit, a man or a woman standing aloof from the thorough and consistent practice of christian virtue and piety, ought to be and will be just as singular and anomalous and reprehensible as a person that should refuse to cultivate his mind, or to get food for his hunger, or to love his kindred and benefactors.

I should have been glad to have gathered and collected the floating remembrances of our old men, of the times and history I have so rapidly passed over. Even now I can seem to see the strife that has marked some portions of the course of the church. But I always turn with grief and humility from records of conflict among christian brethren. The clangor of warfare and heated passion ought never to waken among the sacred echoes of the sanctuary. I would turn from these occasional scenes, not proof indeed of the falsity of our religion or our professions, but evidence of our mortal weakness and passion, to other visions and memories, more constant, more beautiful. The celestial spirit of peace has never long been absent from this society. The failures of christians, the inconsistencies of false brethren, are the exceptions in the course of the church; joy and peace have been the rule. I seem to hear the voice of her many choirs, dissent, he may notify the Clerk thereof, whose duty it shall be to enter the same on record, and such person shall no longer be considered as a member of this Society.

4. We agree to meet at the usual place of holding meetings, in the Academy in Montpelier, on Wednesday, the 27th day of April, instant, at three o'clock in the afternoon, for the purpose of organizing said society with proper officers, and transacting any proper business when met.

Dated at Montpelier, this 12th day of April, 1806.

Elisha Town,
George Worthington,
Joseph Hutchins,
G. B. R. Gove,
Oliver Goss,
Thomas Davis,
Timothy Hubbard,
John Bates,
Charles Bulkley,
Augustus Bradford,
John Hurlbut,
Alden Clark,
Isaac Freeman,
Amasa Brown,
Jeduthan Loomis,
Stuart Boynton,
Willis I. Cadwell,
Abel Wilson,
Phineas Woodbury,
Thomas Reed,
Sylvester Day,
Nathan Jewett,
E. D. Persons,
Samuel Prentiss, jun.
Urial H. Orvis,
Ellis Nye,
Joseph Howes,

Linus Ellis,
William Hutchins,
Jeremiah Wilbur,
Roswell Beckwith,
David Tuthill,
M. B. Billings,
Jonathan Shepherd,
Erastus Watrous,
Silas Burbank,
Cyrus Ware,
Roger Hubbard,
Joseph Freeman,
Edward Lamb,
Nahum Kelton,
Larn'd Lamb,
C. W. Houghton,
Josiah Parks,
Sylvanus Baldwin,
Joseph Wiggins,
Abner H. Powers,
Abel Crooker,
Ebenezer Morse,
Enoch Cheney,
Mason Johnson,
Samuel Goss,
David Edwards,
Elisha Town,
Oliver Dewey,

John Hunt,
Ichabod Peck,
Darius Boyden,
Levi Pitkin,
E. Lewis,
Hers. Estabrooks,
T. Gaylord,
Jude Converse,
Theoph. Pickering,
Archibald Kidd,
Joseph Ray,
Paul Knapp,
Henry Howes,
Samnel West,
D. Edwards, jun.,
Jonathan Edwards,
Aaron Bass,
Charles Hamlin,
William Hamlin,
Timothy Hatch,
Solomon Lewis,
Elijah Tyler,
John Howes,
Joshua Y. Vail,
J. H. Langdon,
S. W. Cobb,
Eben'r Parker.

NAMES OF THE ORIGINAL MEMBERS OF THE CHURCH.

Amasa Brown,
Sylvanus Baldwin,
Andrew Dodge,
Heraldus Estabrooks,
Samuel Goss,
Timothy Hatch,

Joseph Howes,
Solomon Lewis,

Sibyl Brown,
Bachsheba Burbank,
Lydia Davis,

Susanna Lewis,
Lydia Hatch,
Polly Barker,
Patty Howes,
Rebeckah Persons,
Sarah Wiggins.

PASTORS.

Rev. CHESTER WRIGHT, ordained Aug. 16, 1809; dismissed Dec. 22, 1830.
Rev. SAMUEL HOPKINS, ordained Oct. 26, 1831 ; dismissed April 19, 1835.
Rev. BUEL W. SMITH, ordained Aug. 25, 1836; dismissed July 15, 1840.
Rev. JOHN GRIDLEY, installed Dec. 15, 1841 ; dismissed Dec. 9, 1846.
Rev. WM. H. LORD, ordained Sept. 21, 1847.

MEMBERS.

Number of members at the organization,	. .	17
Admitted under Rev. Mr. WRIGHT,	. . .	428
" " Rev. Mr. HOPKINS,	. . .	48
" " stated supply,	. . .	137
" " Rev. Mr. SMITH,	. . .	82
" " Rev. Mr. GRIDLEY,	. . .	46
" " Rev. Mr. LORD,	. . .	166

924